This book
belongs to:

_____

Baby Kermit's New Friends

by
Louise Gikow

· · ·

illustrated by
Lauren Attinello

Muppet Press

For Sandy, Johnny, Paul, and Rachel

—Lauren and Mom

Copyright © 1990 by Henson Associates, Inc.
MUPPET PRESS, MUPPETS, MUPPET BABIES,
and character names are trademarks of Henson Associates, Inc.
All rights reserved, including the right to reproduce this book
or portions thereof in any form.

This 1990 Muppet Press book is published by Longmeadow Press.
Distributed by Checkerboard Press, a division of Macmillan Inc.

Printed in U.S.A.
ISBN 002-689548-X

h g f e d c b a

Ring! Ring! The phone rang in the living room of McDermott the Frog's big old house.

Baby Kermit heard it as he sat in the kitchen, drawing with some new crayons his Great-Uncle McDermott had gotten him.

McDermott poked his head through the doorway. "Kermit? It's for you," he said.

When Kermit picked up the phone, he heard Nanny's voice. It sounded far away.

"I'm sorry, Kermit," she was saying. "But I'm afraid your visit with your great-uncle is going to be longer than we expected. Everyone here has come down with chicken pox, and you can't come home until they're all better."

"How long will that be, Nanny?" Kermit asked, frowning. He already missed his friends, and he'd only been away a few days.

"It could be more than a week," Nanny said. "But I've spoken to your great-uncle, and he's happy to have you stay."

Kermit's lower lip trembled as he hung up the phone. More than a week? A week seemed like forever to be without Piggy and Fozzie and Gonzo and Rowlf and Scooter and Skeeter and Animal.

Great-Uncle McDermott put down his pen and looked over at the little frog. "I'm sorry everyone is sick," he said, "but I'm happy to have you here a little longer. How about a game of checkers?"

"No, thanks," Kermit said. "I don't feel much like checkers right now."

"I can read you a story," Kermit's great-uncle suggested. "Or you can come to the greenhouse with me, and I'll show you some of the baby plants."

Kermit just shook his head. He missed his friends, and he didn't feel like doing much of anything.

Great-Uncle McDermott peered over his spectacles at Kermit. "A walk might do you some good," he suggested gently. "And you can do me a favor. I need some bearberry leaves for my tea. They grow wild out by the O'Bunny place, down past the bend in the river. Just ask for Mr. Gregory O'Bunny. He'll be able to help you." McDermott scratched his head. "You know, it seems to me Gregory has a granddaughter about your age."

But Kermit wasn't very interested.

It was the middle of spring, and the trees were rich and green. Tiny flowers poked up from the damp ground, and the wind whistled a cheerful tune. But Kermit couldn't see the colors, and he didn't hear the music. He was too busy feeling sorry for himself.

Kermit followed the river until he came to a bend. On the other bank, he saw a tiny twig house with a thatched roof. Smoke was drifting out of the chimney.

Kermit was just about to call across for directions when he heard a tiny, squeaky cry. He looked around.

"Help! Somebody help me!"

There, clinging tightly to a rock in the middle of the river, was a little bunny.

"Help! I can't swim!"

Kermit had been swimming since he was a tadpole. He didn't hesitate for a second. He jumped right into the water.

The current was swift, and the water was cold. But Kermit was determined to get to the little bunny. He used the frog kick that Great-Uncle McDermott had taught him the summer before. And finally, he reached the rock.

"Oh, frog," cried the little bunny. "You made it! I was crossing the stream on the old log bridge when it broke free and floated away and I just had time to hop over to this rock but I can't swim and I don't know what I would have done if you hadn't come to rescue me."

She stopped short. "But I still can't swim. How am I going to get home again?" A tiny tear dripped down her bunny nose.

Kermit thought for a moment. Then he had an idea.

"Hop on my back," he told the bunny. "I'll get you home, or my name isn't Kermit."

"I'm Rachel," said the little bunny. "Thank you, Kermit."

With Rachel clinging tightly to his shoulders, Kermit slid into the water again. It was harder going this time, even though Rachel wasn't very heavy. But Kermit knew he could do it.

Finally, Kermit and Rachel reached the bank.

"Thank you again, Kermit," Rachel said gratefully. "If it hadn't been for you, I would have been stuck on that rock past dinnertime and I was already getting hungry and grandfather would have been terribly worried and would you like to come inside? I know grandfather will want to thank you, too."

Inside Rachel's house, it was snug and warm. A little old bunny in waistcoat and spectacles sat in a chair, reading.

"Grandfather!" Rachel called. "This is Kermit and he's a frog and he rescued me when the old log bridge got swept downstream and I was stranded and he came along and... and that's it," Rachel finished, slightly out of breath.

"Thank you for saving Rachel," Rachel's grandfather said, shaking Kermit's hand. Kermit nodded, a little embarrassed. Then he remembered his errand.

"Would you know a Gregory O'Bunny?" he asked. "My Great-Uncle McDermott sent me to find him."

"Why, that's me!" said Rachel's grandfather. He squinted at Kermit. "So you're the nephew McDermott talks about."

"He does?" said Kermit, surprised.

"You bet," said Gregory. "You're his very favorite nephew, you know. It's Kermit this, and Kermit that.... Hey," he went on. "Why don't you both come to dinner tonight?"

Rachel took a deep breath. "I'd really like that, wouldn't you, Kermit? There's plenty of turnip stew and we can play charades later or maybe another game if you don't know charades although I'm sure your uncle must have taught you because he taught me. He's lots of fun, isn't he?"

"Who?" said Kermit.

"Why, your Great-Uncle McDermott, of course!" Rachel said, laughing.

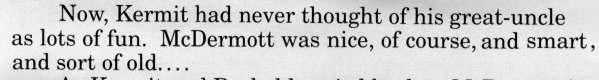

Now, Kermit had never thought of his great-uncle as lots of fun. McDermott was nice, of course, and smart, and sort of old....

As Kermit and Rachel hurried back to McDermott's house, Kermit was silent and thoughtful.

Kermit and Rachel found McDermott in the greenhouse.

"Mr. McDermott?" Rachel shouted happily, giving him a hug. "I met Kermit and he saved me and now Grandfather says come to dinner and could you both please if you don't have other plans?"

"We'd love to," said Great-Uncle McDermott. "That is, if it's all right with you, Kermit."

Kermit just stared. He had never seen anyone hug his uncle.

He had certainly never hugged his uncle.

"Uh, sure," Kermit finally said. "I'd like that." Then he looked curiously at his uncle. "How do you know the O'Bunny family?" he asked.

"Oh, Gregory and I have been friends for a long time," said McDermott. "A while back, I even taught him how to play checkers." McDermott chuckled. "It was a big mistake. Now he beats me all the time."

"Maybe we could play sometime," Rachel said to Kermit.

"You bet," Kermit replied, smiling. Then he turned to his uncle again.

"You know, Uncle McDermott," he said slowly, "I've always thought of you as just my great-uncle. But you taught *me* how to play checkers, too. And you taught me the frog kick and the names of all the flowers, and you always read me stories. You're not only my great-uncle — you're my good friend. Or at least I hope you are. Are you, Uncle McDermott?"

"I'd like to be," Great-Uncle McDermott said quietly. "I know you miss your friends from the nursery. But we can still have a lot of fun while you're here."

Kermit nodded happily. Then, a little shyly, he gave his great-uncle a hug.

That night, Kermit had a wonderful time at the O'Bunnys'. He played charades and blind bunny's bluff, and Rachel beat him three times at checkers. By the time the evening was over, he and Rachel were becoming good friends.

But his best new friend of all was his Great-Uncle McDermott.